BUNNY
Figures It Out

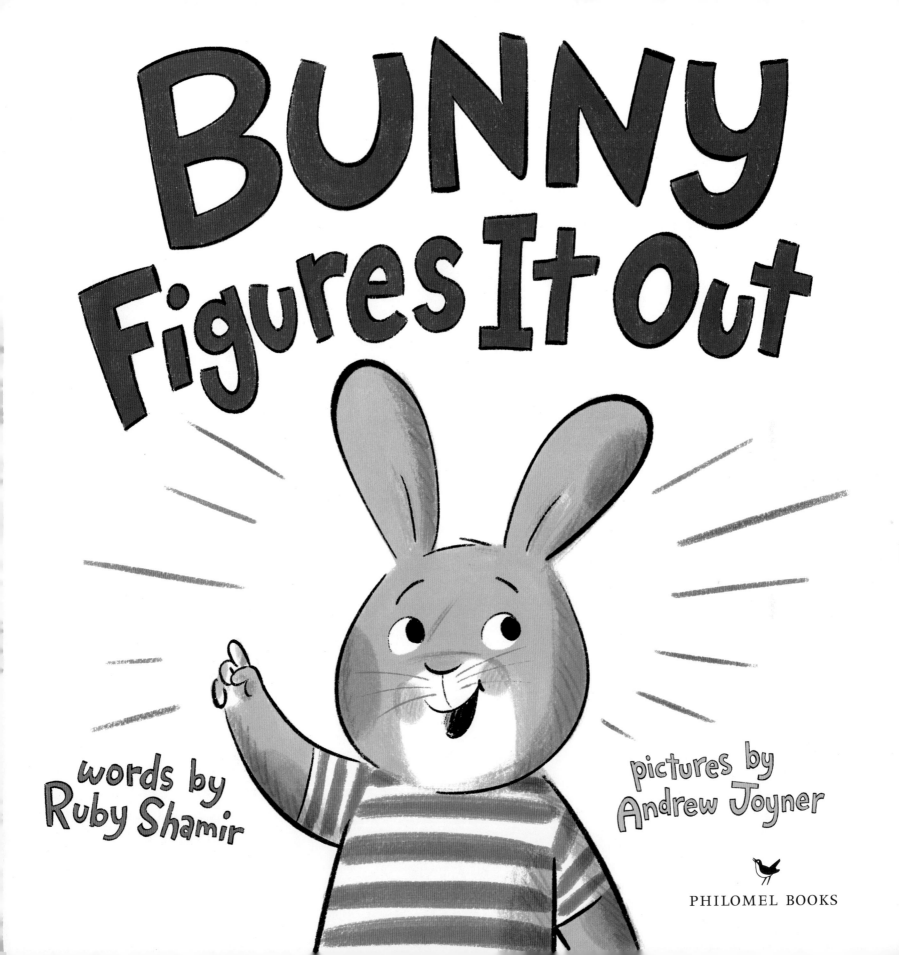

words by
Ruby Shamir

pictures by
Andrew Joyner

PHILOMEL BOOKS

Bunny had been waiting for lunch since breakfast. She knew exactly what she wanted. Soft, chewy bread; thick, rich peanut butter; and most importantly: grape jelly. Sweet, and sticky, and perfectly purple.

But when she reached into the fridge for the jelly jar, she discovered it was empty. No sweetness. No stickiness. No purpleness either. What was a bunny to do?

Frantically, Bunny searched everywhere.
Inside the cupboards, under the table,
behind the chairs. She even poked her
head in the hamper. No luck.

"Mom!" she yelled. "There's no grape jelly!"

"Sorry, honey," her mom called back. "We'll get some more at the store next time we go."

"What's peanut butter without jelly?" Bunny grumbled at her half-made sandwich.

Then she had an idea.

"What if I make grape jelly?"

There was just one problem:
Bunny had no idea how to do that.

But Bunny's big brother knew how to do lots of things. "I'll just ask Jack," she figured.

Bunny hopped in front of her brother's video game.

"Do you know how to make grape jelly?" she asked.

"Huh? No. I'll check my phone," Jack said.

He swiftly tapped a few words onto his phone, tossed it to Bunny, and returned to his game.

Bunny clicked on the first thing she saw: "Grape Jelliez."

"It's a pair of purple sandals," she said.

"Huh?" Jack answered.

"Never mind," Bunny muttered.

Her brother had been no help at all.
But then she had a new idea.

"I bet Kitty will know! She's the best student in our class."

Bunny hopped over to her neighbor's house and knocked on the door.

"Do you know how to make grape jelly?" Bunny asked.

"Oh yes," Kitty said, scribbling on a slip of paper. "Put a bunch of grapes in a bowl, sprinkle them with glitter, and twirl around three times saying these magic words." She handed the note to Bunny.

"Are you sure?" Bunny asked.

"Positive," Kitty answered. "I saw it in a video."

"Okay." Bunny shrugged and hopped home.

Back in her kitchen, Bunny pulled a bowl of grapes from the refrigerator and poured some glitter over them. She stretched her arms and spun.

"Bibbley, Bebbley, fill my belly. Jibbley, Jebbley, send forth jelly!" Bunny chanted.

Bunny looked in the bowl. No jelly. But she refused to give up.

"Someone's got to know how to make grape jelly. I think I
need to ask a grown-up."

Bunny hopped back outside and saw her dad working on the car.

"Dad, do you know how to make grape jelly?" she asked.

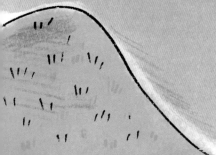

"Isn't grape jelly just squished-up grapes and sugar?" her dad called out.

"Right!" Bunny exclaimed. "I'll give that a try."

Bunny washed the glitter off her grapes and laid them down on the patio. She poured some sugar over them.

Bunny's heart raced with excitement as she hopped on her bike. Soon she'd have the stickiest, sweetest, most perfectly purple jelly around!

Bunny sped over the grapes.

But when she turned to look back at the patio, she didn't see any jelly. All she saw was a mess. And now she was really, really hungry!

"Does anyone know how to make grape jelly??" Bunny cried.

Suddenly, another idea popped into Bunny's head.
"I should ask Grandma!" Bunny decided. "I love
her food best."

Bunny hopped over to the senior center, where Grandma
was in the middle of a heated game of dominoes.

"Hi, Grandma!" Bunny greeted her with a kiss. "Do you know how to make grape jelly?"

"Of course, sweetheart," Grandma said. "I used to make jelly with my own grandmother back in the day. Here's what you do."

Bunny took out a pen and paper and started writing as Grandma spoke. "You start with fresh fruit, a squeeze of lemon, and then—"

"Excuse me, that's not how you make grape jelly," said one of Grandma's friends. "You need to mix grapes in a pot with simple syrup and—"

"Are you kidding?" Grandma's other friend piped in. "Never use syrup in jelly! You always use plain white sugar first and then—"

Bunny looked up at Grandma and her friends arguing, then she looked down at her piece of paper. Everyone was giving her different instructions. Bunny sighed and slumped out the door, her tummy rumbling.

Why was it so hard to find someone who knew how to make grape jelly?

As she headed home, Bunny passed by the library. She remembered how the librarian at her school always helped find answers to her questions—like why is the grass green? What makes boats float? And how hot is the sun? Maybe this librarian could help her now.

Bunny went in and took a deep breath. "Excuse me,"
she asked, "do you know how to make grape jelly?"

"I don't," the librarian said. Bunny's heart sank right down to her toes.

"But," she added, "I know how you can find out. Come with me!"

The librarian led Bunny to a huge bookshelf.

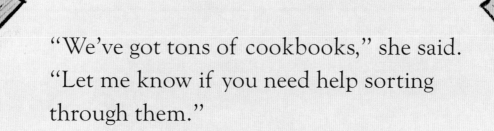

"We've got tons of cookbooks," she said. "Let me know if you need help sorting through them."

There was a whole row about jelly!

One book in particular caught Bunny's eye: *The Jelly Test Kitchen*.
Bunny read page after page until she landed on just the thing: "Our
chefs tested dozens of recipes and this is the one for the stickiest,
sweetest, and most perfectly purple grape jelly!"

"Yes!" Bunny jumped up. "This is
what I've been looking for all day!"

As Bunny checked out the book, she hugged the librarian. Then she sprinted out the door, book in hand, and raced back home.

"Look!"

"No glitter, huh?" Kitty marveled.

"No glitter at all!" Bunny said.

Just sweet and sticky and perfectly purple grape jelly.

How to Make Grape Jelly

After testing lots of recipes, the best (and simplest) grape jelly recipe I found came from a box of pectin, the ingredient that makes the jelly gel. I'm including it here so that anyone looking for a grape jelly recipe (like Bunny) can find it in the library. You can make jelly out of many different fruits—even hot pepper! Depending on which fruit you use, the recipe will be a little different. I used regular red grapes that I got at the supermarket. You'll need help from a grown-up because this recipe calls for cooking on the stove.

INGREDIENTS

1½ pounds of red grapes without their stems

⅛ cup of lemon juice

½ cup of water

2 teaspoons of pectin (I used Pomona's Universal Pectin)

1 cup of sugar (you can use as little as a half a cup of sugar)

2 teaspoons of calcium water (the powder to make it came with the pectin)

TOOLS

Heavy-bottomed pot • Potato masher • Heatproof bowl or pitcher • Strainer or colander • Cheesecloth • Mixing bowl

INSTRUCTIONS

1. Wash grapes and pull them off the stem.

2. Place grapes in pot with lemon juice and water and simmer for about 10–20 minutes. As the grapes soften, mash them with a potato masher. Add a little more water if the grapes start to stick to the bottom of the pot.

3. Set up the bowl or pitcher with a colander or strainer on top and line the strainer with cheesecloth.

4. After the grapes are cooked and well mashed, pour them into the cheesecloth and let the juice drain into the bowl until it stops dripping. One and a half pounds of stemmed grapes should produce 2 cups of juice.

5. Mix the pectin and the sugar together in a separate bowl.

6. Pour the 2 cups of juice back into the pot and add the calcium water.

7. Bring the juice to a full boil, then add the pectin and sugar mixture and stir energetically for 1–2 minutes so that the mixture dissolves while it all returns to a full boil. Turn off the stove.

8. Pour into a heatproof bowl, let cool, and enjoy!

If you want to preserve the jelly, you have to get canning jars with special lids and follow instructions to make sure the jelly is safely preserved.

To my best bunnies: Dante, Allegra, and Romy. And to Nicky, always. —R.S.

For Jane, Ian, and Mia. —A.J.

PHILOMEL BOOKS
An imprint of Penguin Random House LLC, New York

First published in the United States of America by Philomel, an imprint of Penguin Random House LLC, 2021.

Text copyright © 2021 by Ruby Shamir. • Illustrations copyright © 2021 by Andrew Joyner.

Library of Congress Cataloging-in-Publication Data is available. • Manufactured in China.

ISBN 9780593115282

1 3 5 7 9 10 8 6 4 2

Edited by Jill Santopolo. • Design by Monique Sterling. • Text set in Goudy Old Style.